SWEET
Lorraine

ARTHUR H. VEASEY III

For Helen and Bobby

Chapter 1

THE BIRDWATCHER

The hiker ambled along the narrow path that bordered the river's edge and dense woods, before stopping to gaze across the bulrush that occupied a long, sweeping bend in the river where the current subsided and waterfowl found friendly breeding grounds. She had been here many times before; her eyes leaped from one familiar view to another. Wood ducks and shrike were common amid the shallow tidal basins, but she was a birder on the hunt for something less common—the snowy egret, renowned for its white plumage, black legs, and yellow feet—and she was eager to catch one of these nesting creatures in the lens of her new, German-made binoculars.

A breeze fanned her face as morning mist dissipated into sunshine, and a sudden splash betrayed a common crane, a swift dart of its beak snatching a minnow from the inlet and down its slender throat. She smiled, then aimed her field glasses to an area beyond, where she thought the habitat more favorable.

Her vision swept across the marsh, alternating between lens and the naked eye, until something caught her attention among the weeds about fifty feet away, a peculiar object protruding from the slack tide, something foreign and indistinct. As she rotated the focusing ring, the magnification produced a clearer view of the object. A moment passed, before a sudden and involuntary gasp rendered the woman breathless. "Oh my God," she whispered.

As she sprinted down the path, retracing her morning trek, her binoculars swung recklessly, banging against the woman's arms and chest, yet she hardly took notice while she raced toward her car, parked near the road. Hands trembling, she raised her key ring to the steering column, before it fell to the floorboard. "Shit!" she exclaimed. Grabbing the key chain again, she jammed the key into the ignition, turned the engine over, threw it into gear, and sped off, spewing gravel in her rapid flight.

.   .   .

At the West Newbury police barracks, Charlie Bevins was already on duty. He had been chief of police for almost two years and had yet to confront anything more challenging than a few nasty domestic incidents. Law enforcement more often involved underage-drinking episodes that usually culminated in a stern warning and a call to the parents, rather than anywhere near a jail cell.

He sipped his coffee and was looking over the log from the previous night, when he saw a familiar car swerve pell-mell into the parking lot. The driver leaped from the vehicle and made a dash for the office, before Charlie intercepted her at the doorway.

"Carrie, what the heck are you doing driving in here like that?" The woman was breathless, and her face was flushed. "What's the matter? Are you all right?"

"Oh, Charlie, you have to come now. You won't believe what I've just seen."

.   .   .

Nick Ridgeway was the product of a prosperous New England family. His Puritan ancestors had arrived in the New World around 1650 and, like most everyone else, had called farming their occupation through five generations, before his great-grandfather had come down from the hills of New Hampshire to take up the trade of stair building. Dennis Ridgeway had been not just a tradesman but an artisan who had created beautiful stairways in some of the most elegant buildings and homes in nineteenth-century Boston, Worcester, and Providence. Nick prized a set of carpentry planes that he had inherited; from the leveling planes to the jack planes to the smoothing planes, they exemplified an obligation to skill, discipline, and an honest day's work—what his family always referred to as the Protestant ethic.

A generation later, it was Nick's grandfather who struck the family fortune. Through hard work, an industrious nature, and some measure of good luck, he came to own one of the largest woolen mills in New England, producing more flannel than any other textile firm in America. The textile industry eventually moved south, and the mills were no longer a family enterprise by the time Nick was born, but the piety devoted to hard work and attainment was in the bloodline. He set off to Dartmouth to prepare himself for law school but soon found that he liked examining the intricacies of everyday life more than he did legal treatises, so it seemed very natural to him that he should transfer to Middlebury and learn how to write. After graduation and with paternal faith, his father said he would support him for a year or so, until he might secure gainful employment as a writer. After three months as an unpaid gofer for the *Union Leader* in Manchester, New Hampshire, Nick got his first break when the newspaper guild insisted the paper either fire or hire the kid amid a hotly contested gubernatorial election. He worked there for the next eight years, before coming home to the *Daily News* to serve as a staff reporter, columnist, and now managing editor.

He was stationed at his usual post on the city desk on a Wednesday when the call came in from Jade Lash.

"Nick, I'm at the West Newbury Police Department. A body was discovered in the river about a mile or so downstream from the Rocks Village Bridge. Some birdwatcher with sharp eyes stumbled on it this morning."

Jade was without any doubt the best reporter at the paper—she had a nose for news, and she was dogged in her pursuit of story lines that others overlooked. She had worked with Ridgeway for nearly ten years and should have been promoted to editor long ago, but it was a man's world and she accepted that. Besides, she liked news gathering from the field. That was lucky for Nick. "They couldn't get to the corpse by boat because of the tide, and the mudflats are impassable from the shore this time of year. So the fire department got called in, and they laid down a track of ladders end to end so that two of their guys could crawl out on their hands and knees and drag the body ashore. A very slow and messy process."

"Any description of the victim?"

"Not yet—from what I've heard, the body is badly decomposed, and some of its limbs are missing."

"Okay, you stick with it, kiddo. I'll see what I can find out from this end." Ridgeway pressed the switch hook, then tucked the receiver between his jawbone and his shoulder as he dialed.

"State Police. Sergeant Murphy speaking."

"Sergeant, this is Nick Ridgeway at the *Daily News*. I'm calling to find out if you have any open missing-persons reports for Essex County that were filed in the last twelve months."

"Hold on—let me look at the case sheets." He could hear the shuffling of papers, then silence for a minute, before the voice came back on the line. "I have three: Michael Basile, forty-four-year-old male, Peabody, missing since August tenth; Gloria Donahue, fifty-year-old female, Lynn, missing since December twenty-eighth; and Alvin Parker, Jr., twenty-nine-year-old male, Amesbury, missing since April eleventh."

Nick wrote down the information, thanked the trooper, and circled the last name on the list.

Jade returned to the office around one o'clock with a brown-bag lunch, tuna on rye, which she shared with Nick while he filled her in on the missing-persons list. "I found this news brief from last April on the Parker disappearance; his father reported him as a walkout, nothing more. What do we know about our John Doe?"

"Very little so far. They sent the body to the state medical examiner in Lawrence. We should have the pathology report next week. But get this: the fireman I talked to said that it looked like there was some kind of heavy cord wrapped around the ankle, but that was all he would say. I asked if it was a man or a woman, and apparently he couldn't tell from all the decomposition.

He did say that the body looked like it had been in the water for at least six months."

"That would put our John Doe in the river before Alvin Parker went missing—but maybe, maybe not. The cord makes it sound like it could be some kind of a gangland hit. I'll follow up on that angle. You dig around the local side of things—interview Parker's family to see if they have any theories on his disappearance, and find out if he was married. We can wait on the pathology report until we start looking elsewhere."

.   .   .

The house at 359 Main Street was a plain, gable-front cottage with two bow windows on the first floor and its back to the river, snubbing the bright tidal waters of the Merrimack, a common characteristic of many nineteenth-century homes in Amesbury. Jade looked at her notepad to confirm she had the right address before knocking on the door. The man who answered, Alvin Parker, Sr., was average height and looked fit for a man in his late fifties. A lineman for the Amesbury Electric Company, he had lived in the area for most of his adult life; he and his wife had raised their only child, Alvin, Jr., there. A phone call that he had received from a local newspaper that afternoon had prepared him for his visitor.

"I'm glad to meet you, Miss Lash, and I'm especially anxious to know if the body that they found in the river is my son. I pray that it's not, but I need answers."

"I understand your anxiety, Mr. Parker. That's one of the reasons why I'm here. But the authorities won't be able to give further forensic details of the remains until a full autopsy has been performed. We should know something in the next forty-eight hours."

"I've waited this long. I can wait a couple more days, I guess." His eyes were moist as he stared out the window at the Merrimack. This was the hard part of the job, those awkward moments when you had to interject your nosy self into the privacy of survivors—families and loved ones who would carry the heartache long after the reporters had moved on to their next assignment.

"Let's start with a couple of questions."

Parker returned his eyes to his inquisitor and nodded soberly.

"When did you last see your son?"

"Two days before he disappeared. He stopped by to pick up some electrical supplies that he needed. He was repairing some old motorboats at the shop that he built next to the cottage up on Lake Attitash. He had big plans to open a boat rental service this summer to make a few extra bucks and maybe pave the way for some other lakefront business ventures."

Like most reporters, Jade had her own unschooled method of shorthand and hurriedly scratched out a few symbols in her notebook.

"That was the last I saw of him. He never showed up for work on Monday, and that's not like him. Al loved his job at Hytron and was as reliable an employee as you could possibly find—and that's a fact, Miss Lash!"

"What happened next?"

"Well, I asked Lorraine—that's his wife—what she knew, and she told me that they'd had a fight, a disagreement, really, and that he'd left her in a huff. So we all figured he'd gone someplace to let off some steam and that eventually he'd cool down and come home. I couldn't figure out where he might have gone, but I was pretty sure he'd show up sooner or later. But by Wednesday I began to worry, so I went down to the police station and filed a missing-persons report. Five days later, they found Al's car abandoned at an MTA parking lot in Everett." Parker pursed his lips and shook his head absently.

Jade let the silence hang in the room for a few seconds before probing further. "You mentioned your son's wife, Lorraine. What can you tell me about her?"

"Lorraine? Why, Lorraine and Al were high school sweethearts. They got married right after they graduated, in 1944. It was probably too soon, but the war was still on and Al got called up to serve, so they did what a lot of young kids did in those days: they eloped before his deployment."

"What did she do while he was gone?"

"She continued to live at home with her parents across town. We'd see her only now and again, but I remember she had a part-time job at the department store downtown and did some babysitting. Mostly she stayed home and waited for Al to return, which he did after V-J Day, when the military demobilization got him an early discharge from the Navy."

Jade paused to write down a few more notes, before glancing up again. "You mentioned Hytron Laboratories in Newburyport. How long did he work there?"

"He got the job about two years ago. It seemed like an ideal situation at the time. You see, Al always wanted to go to college to study electrical engineering, but the war, marriage, and three kids got in the way of that. Anyway, at Hytron he worked in the television tube department, a really good fit with his aptitude for electronics, and there seemed to be a chance for advancement. But he wound up supervising the night shift while Lorraine waited tables at a diner in Merrimac during the daytime to help make ends meet. In my mind, it was no way to have a healthy relationship. If they were lucky, they had one night a week to do things together like most husbands and wives, but the rest of the week—kaput."

"Do you think that led to marital difficulties?"

"That's hard for me to say, but she did file for divorce after his disappearance, charging him with pain and mental anguish. I thought that maybe once he got wind of that he'd come flying home, but . . ." His voice trailed off, and Jade could see that he was emotionally spent. They chatted amiably for a few more minutes, before she held out her hand and thanked him for his time. As he walked her to the door, he said, "Just do me one favor, Miss Lash: don't let nobody whitewash this case. I'm no detective, but if you ask me, there's more going on here than meets the eye."

Chapter 2

THE CRIME LAB

Two days after the body was discovered, Dr. Stuart Manikas, of Harvard Medical School, arrived at the Massachusetts State Police Crime Lab facilities in Lawrence, where the county medical examiner, Harold Levine, received him. The two men had worked together on previous occasions, so they kept their greetings cordial but brief, then entered the examination room.

The clinicians went through a standard questionnaire, checking off preexamination protocol in rapid succession before starting the autopsy. The body was naked, marked only by a plain paper toe tag, and Manakis began with a close visual inspection of the corpse. Speaking matter-of-factly, he delivered the postmortem exercise as Levine transcribed his findings.

"No noticeable scars or tattoos. Hair and eye color difficult to determine, due to diffusion and lividity of the skin, head, and scalp. Torso exhibits severe contusions. Left leg is dismembered below the knee; right hand is dismembered at the wrist". Both exhibit contributory evidence of rapid decomposition, as opposed to blunt-force trauma."

Next, they weighed and measured the body, which was swollen and billowed after months of submersion. Without instruction, Levine maneuvered the torso onto a rubber block and Manikas adroitly performed a Y-shaped incision that allowed for inspection of the internal organs. "The lungs show no sign of water inhalation. Let's get a look at the nasal cavity and larynx to see if they're plugged." After several minutes of dissection, he declared softly, "No conclusive evidence of dry drowning, either." Neither man displayed surprise; the diagnosis of drowning could pose problems because the findings were often minimal, obscure, or, as in this case, absent.

"Let's get a closer look at the skull," Manikas said. He checked behind the ears and the back of the head, before directing his attention to the face. Profoundly disfigured by the elements of the river, it was masticated and scabby. He used his fore and middle fingers to systematically explore the anterior of the head from forehead to chin, until his hand stopped moving. "Well, now, what do we have here?" A dimple just below the orbit of the right eye exposed an area of facial distress. He probed further with his forceps, until they revealed a small but deep injury that experience told him was consistent with a gunshot wound. Methodically moving his hands around to the back of the skull, he found what he was searching for: an exit wound near the muscular part of the neck. He looked up at Levine. "It appears to be a near-contact gunshot wound. Let's see if there's more." Moving his fingers laterally from the right ear, he stopped abruptly. "Bingo!" The second wound was squarely at the victim's temple. Manikas used his dissector and forceps to probe deeply into the brain tissue until he found and removed the bullet.

Levine stared at the flattened slug. "It has to be another close-range gunshot, Stuart. I'm guessing a twenty-two-caliber pistol."

Manikas nodded. "Let's see what else we might find." Thirty minutes later, the two men had completed their examination. In addition to the gunshot wounds, they discovered two nonlethal stab wounds to the thorax. The gunshot to the temporal bone was determined to be cause of death.

Before they could complete the autopsy, protocol called for the victim's fingerprints to be taken. Manikas frowned as he surveyed the surviving hand. "It's badly compromised, Harry, and the skin is shriveled. Let's see if we can improvise here a little bit."

Levine looked on as his colleague adeptly cut the skin on one barely intact finger. He carefully slid his own finger in, underneath the pallid skin, and smoothed it out from the inside. "Okay, see what you can get." Using a small roller, Levine inked the digit, then pressed it to a fingerprint pad. He attached the evidence to the report and held it up for Manikas to see. "Not a bad result." He smiled. "I think we're done."

Before submitting the report to the DA, Levine listed separately, as a customary addendum, several other nonforensic observations, including the remnants of what appeared to be a maroon corduroy shirt that had been found on the victim. Directly below, he made the notation "nb": every medical school student's abbreviation for the Latin phrase *nota bene*. Next it to he wrote, "Left leg bound with electrical wire."

.   .   .

It was Sunday, and the second game of a doubleheader at Fenway was softly broadcasting through the half-deserted second-floor newsroom. Malzone was batting in the bottom of the fifth, with Piersall on deck. Nick was a baseball guy, and the sound of the play-by-play announcer's warm, gravelly voice over the airwaves was soothing to his eardrums, even if he was only half listening. The old place was a second home, grubby with tobacco smoke and metal dust that wafted up from the Linotypes. His workstation, a desk in a cluster of four, had an ashtray, a half-eaten bagel from the luncheonette next door, and stacks of paper everywhere that made the place as much a firetrap as a workplace. He was assiduously editing the Monday-morning edition when the phone interrupted his stream of consciousness.

"Ridgeway."

"Ha! I figured I'd catch you in the newsroom—home is where the typewriter is, I guess." Jade's voice, low and husky, was spirited, as always. She liked needling him because she knew it was the printer's ink in his blood that kept him in the newsroom at all hours of the day. On her long list of friends and lovers, Nick was the only man she had ever completely trusted. He was both mentor and confidant and always plainspoken. She had been head over heels for him at one time, but the half-your-age-plus-seven rule had stuck in his head, so they had never done anything about it.

"Someone has to keep the planet informed. What's up?"

"I was at the two o'clock Mass at St. Joe's, where I ran into one of my friends from the DA's office. He told me, on the QT, that a fingerprint taken from the body at the morgue is a match with our Alvin Parker."

"I'll be damned," Ridgeway whispered.

"Not only that, but they found two bullet holes in the late Mr. Parker's skull."

Leaning forward, he pulled out his last Marlboro and lit it, before crumpling the pack and missing its intended target, as it came to rest on the floor next to the wastebasket.

"Well, now, I guess we have a local murder mystery on our hands after all. Make sure you get in here early tomorrow so I can juggle assignments. I'll put somebody else on city council. I'm going to need your full attention to chase down more than a few angles on this fish story. But first things first—circle back to your contact at the DA's office and see what you can learn about the cord that the fireman found attached to the body's leg. It's sounds like the corpse might have been weighed down in an attempt to keep it submerged. Then get in touch with the harbormaster to see if he can help us figure out just how far a body could theoretically travel downriver in the course of a spring freshet. I'm sure we'll require more help with this little equation, but it's a good starting point.

"I'm on it, Boss."

"And one more thing—don't let Moynihan know you're sticking your nose into this."

.   .   .

Red Moynihan was the chief of police in Amesbury, a high-minded cop whose reputation as a straight arrow meant he did things by the book. He was raised in a strict Catholic family, the seventh of ten children, and early on determined to plot his own course, in spite of the fact that he had lots of brothers and sisters looking after him. He was a popular student and a natural leader; his mother wanted him to become a priest, but the idea of long robes and celibacy never appealed to his inner self, even though he never married. He had plenty of chances, mind you, but whoever was going to lasso Red Moynihan was going to have to be something special, and he never quite found that girl of his dreams. By now he was a man's man: he coached baseball and canoed and fished at his cabin in Maine, where he guided a group of ten high school boys along the Allagash Wilderness Waterway for two weeks every summer with his two springer spaniels. The long and short of it was that he was too set in his ways for married life, and law enforcement was now the epicenter of his professional career.

He growled when he saw Nick entering police headquarters. "I know why you're here, Ridgeway, and I've got nothing for you. The state police are handling this investigation, and until they declare it a homicide and ask for my assistance, my hands are tied."

"Well, I'm pretty sure you read the coroner's report, Red. One bullet to the head, and you might guess suicide, but two slugs? Sure sounds like murder to me."

"Ask me no questions, I'll tell you no lies."

"Well, how about a discussion of the facts as we know them? Alvin Parker's father said that five days after he reported his son missing, the kid's car was found abandoned in Everett. Did anybody follow up on that lead to see if there was any evidence of foul play?"

"The car's been impounded, and we're examining it now. That's all I can say."

"I hear that the body had some kind of electrical wire bound to it. It seems like it might have been weighed down before it was thrown into the river. Have you thought about dispatching a team of divers to look for more evidence?"

"And where would you suggest we start the search? There are sixteen miles of waterway from Haverhill to Newburyport. The body could have entered the Merrimack at any spot before or during the spring surge."

"Well, the Rocks Village Bridge might be a logical start."

"You can be sure our investigation will cover all possibilities."

"Does that include the possibility of organized criminal activity?"

"Not unless you know something we don't. The decedent had a clean record and, as far as we know, no vices. Should you find evidence to the contrary, please feel free to bring it to our attention." Moynihan was playing poker, but Nick didn't want to overplay his hand, either, so he thanked him for his time and left the station. Moynihan was probably right about the victim's record, he thought, but there was something about this case that made Nick want to dig deeper.

.   .   .

Like all good newshounds, Nick had a long list of sources. Some were insiders, people who could give you the skinny on what was going on behind closed doors at city hall or the gossip circulating around the squad room. But in the darker recesses of humanity, you needed something a little less sanitary—a snitch, an informant with ties to the underworld who could tell the wise guys from the small-time hoodlums, someone with an ear to the ground when it came to the business of gangland rivalry. Around the Merrimack Valley, if a corpse was suspected to be the victim of Sicilian justice, Eddie Cook was the guy you consulted if you wanted scuttlebutt. Eddie's father, Michael Kukis, immigrated from Lithuania in 1936, changed his name to Cook, enlisted in the army, and was killed on a battlefield in Belgium. As a result, Eddie was raised fatherless in the Acre section of Haverhill, surviving with a quick wit and even quicker hands if it came down to a street fight.

Nick was a reporter for the *Union Leader* when he helped Eddie out of a jam after he was arrested for nearly pummeling to death a shoe-factory foreman who was sexually abusing Eddie's mother. After Nick did a feature story on the case, the DA dropped the charges. Eddie never forgot the gesture and remained in his debt. The two men met at the Shoe City Tavern and, after a couple of beers, got down to business.

"I seen your story in the paper about this Parker guy, Nick. It ain't nothin' I know about. But, shit, if every stiff that came floatin' down the river was a mob hit, I'd be outta business." Eddie chuckled. "I mean, the Irish have been loan-sharking this side of the Merrimack for years. Long as they stay outta my way, there's no hard feelings and no turf wars."

"So, no vendettas or bad blood, eh?" Nick prodded.

"No, nothing like that, but . . ." Eddie paused for a moment.

"Go on," Nick urged him.

"So, there's this guy who starts showin' up at the Hampton Beach Casino with an entourage last summer—a real sharpie, well dressed, wears a Panama hat and a linen suit. Everybody calls him the Baron, like he's some kind of royalty or somethin'. Well, there was this incident one night—Artie Flynn . . . You know Artie?"

Nick nodded no.

"Artie's a local kid, a wannabe wise guy, and a real Romeo with the ladies. Anyway, Artie walks into the casino and finds this Baron guy makin' time with a broad half his age, a real looker, girl next door type. Artie goes over, and a few choice words are exchanged, if you know what I mean. A lot of swagger goes down before one of the Baron's henchmen whacks Artie upside the head and he bolts the place. Next thing I know, he's back with half the fuckin' Hibernian army and a brawl breaks out. I don't have no dog in this fight, so I'm layin' low, when I spy the Baron sidestepping punches and escorting Cinderella out the front door like he's Prince Charming."

"Interesting story, but what does this have to do with my investigation?"

"The dame with the glass slipper—her name's Lorraine Parker. I think she's married to your floater."

Chapter 3

THE INVESTIGATION

A week went by before Jade could arrange a rendez-vous with her contact. Frank Rizzo was a state police lieutenant attached to the district attorney's office and one of the first law enforcement officials to have interviewed Lorraine Parker after the body was positively identified as that of her husband, Alvin. Jade and Frank had known each other since high school days and had a long-standing mutual trust when it came to sharing information.

"At first she wouldn't believe it. But when I explained to her that the fingerprint we collected was an exact match with Parker's Navy records and told her about the maroon corduroy shirt that her mother-in-law identified, she came around and began to talk. She told me that on the night of April tenth, they had a quarrel, during which he abused and struck her so severely that her chin bled. They fought continually until finally she locked him out of the house and went to bed. She doesn't know where he went after that but says she never saw him again. Sometime after his disappearance, she closed the cottage and moved in with her parents, before filing for divorce."

"What was the argument about?"

"She hated her job waitressing at the diner in Merrimac. She really wanted to be at home, taking care of the kids and playing housewife, but they needed the extra dough. Parker's job at Hytron didn't pay enough, and she says he spent too much time dreaming up get-rich-quick schemes that went nowhere. She definitely longed for the finer things in life, which Parker couldn't provide. The cottage at the lake was another bone of contention. The place is pretty cold and desolate during the winter months, and by April she'd had enough of it. She told him she was ready to move back to civilization. I guess that's what finally set him off."

"Any evidence that ties her to his murder?"

"No, nothing conclusive. The crime lab went through the car top to bottom, and even though they found traces of blood in the trunk, it wasn't enough to come up with a definitive match, and Parker hunted so it could have been animal blood. But here's where it gets interesting: the lab guys said the inside had been recently scrubbed clean with a disinfectant."

"That seems suspicious."

"Enough that we're requesting that the Amesbury Police Department send a forensics team out to Lake Attitash to scour the area for any other evidence of a crime."

"What else do you have for me?"

"You ready for more grisly details? After the body was retrieved, we sent a photographer down to the location near River Road to take some pictures. There, in the soggy marsh, he discovered the left leg of the dismembered body. Electrical wire wrapped around the ankle matched that found on the cadaver."

"Do you think the body was dumped there?"

"Not likely. It was too remote, and the remains were too far offshore. Our thinking is that the victim was most likely discharged a mile or two upstream. The local harbormaster figures there's enough unobstructed current through that stretch to drag the remains that distance or more."

"So, the Rocks Village Bridge could easily have been the launching place Alvin Parker's assailants used to dispose of the body."

"Sure, but it would have to have been carried out under cover of darkness. If it had been daytime, there would have been too great a chance of being observed."

"Any ideas about a motive?'

"We don't speculate on that. Our job is to collect the forensic evidence where we find it, and present it to the DA. The ball is in Moynihan's court for the local gumshoes to figure out the whodunnit part of this puzzle."

.   .   .

Red Moynihan got the call he had expected ever since the case had been declared a homicide. The DA wanted the Amesbury PD to assist the state police in the search for evidence at the Parker cottage at Lake Attitash. It was standard procedure to engage local law enforcement to investigate a local crime scene where a murder was involved, and it was not unusual to view a spouse as a potential suspect and canvass the home for evidence that might shed light on the killer and any possible motive for the slaying. Still, Moynihan had mixed feelings. He knew Lorraine Parker's parents, and he saw her infrequently when she worked at the department store on Main Street. She was one of those pretty and charming girls, born as if by fate to an ordinary middle-class family. She dressed plainly because she had never been able to afford anything better, but she possessed indisputable refinement, as if her beauty, grace, and natural charm had taken the place of birth and family. And when you talked with her, she looked at you openly, with a gaze that exuded warmth, sincerity, and attentiveness.

It was pouring rain when he arrived at Lake Attitash with two of his field team inspectors early the next morning. The cottage was a one-and-a-half-story bungalow with a low pitched roof. A broad porch gave access to the front door, which opened directly into the living room's informal interior and open floor plan. Lorraine was waiting and admitted the men through the front door.

"Good morning, Chief Moynihan. It's nice to see you again."

"Always a pleasure to see you, Lorraine. I'm sorry for your loss."

"Yes, thank you. All of this has come as a tremendous shock, as you can imagine. But it's so much water under the bridge, as they say. Now, how can I help you with your assignment?"

"As the district attorney probably told you, we're here to inspect the cottage for any physical evidence that might shed light on your husband's death."

"Oh my."

"I can assure you that our detectives will work quietly and efficiently in the course of this investigation while they examine the condition of the cottage and the property inside."

"How long will this take?"

"It will begin with an initial walk-through, so that the detectives can get a general feel for the layout and at the same time conduct a visual examination, after which they'll document their findings by drawing sketches of the rooms and taking photographs of anything that they think may be useful as evidence. As for any physical evidence that may be collected, it will be tagged, logged, securely packaged, and receipted before it is sent to the state crime lab. The process from start to finish will take up most of the day."

"This all sounds so daunting," she responded, wide-eyed. "Well, then, I suppose your detectives had best begin."

Moynihan nodded at the two men, who withdrew to the next room to initiate the inspection. He turned back to Lorraine and said, "While they do their work, it would be helpful if I could ask a few questions."

"By all means, ask me anything at all."

"Did your husband own any firearms?"

"Yes, he had several—at least two shotguns and a hunting rifle. The shotguns should be in the cellar, and he kept his hunting rifle in a storage case in the closet in our bedroom."

"Do you recall if he owned any handguns?"

"Hmm, I'm not sure. I remember that I saw him with a pistol once, but I don't know if it was his or if it belonged to Artie Flynn."

"Who is Artie Flynn?"

"Artie used to work with Al at Hytron." Moynihan didn't need his notepad; his memory for such details was keen, and he filed this information instantly in the back of his head. He didn't know Artie from Adam's off ox, but when it came to guns, Moynihan would leave no stone unturned—Artie Flynn, whoever he was, would receive a full background check.

"You told Lieutenant Rizzo that you and Al had a fight on the eve of his disappearance, didn't you?"

"Yes, we quarreled over a number of things, mostly money. We've been married for ten years, and all we have to show for it is this drab old cottage and a beat-up convertible."

"And did he strike you at any time during this particular argument?"

"He pushed me aside and knocked me to the floor. I fell facefirst and cut my chin on the hardwood floor. I don't think he meant to do it, but he was angry and his temper got the best of him, I guess."

"What happened next?"

"Well, I was crying uncontrollably, and he shook me and kept yelling at me to stop. Finally, he stepped outside to cool off. That's when I locked him out. I was afraid he would kick in the door, but he just drove off. It was the last I ever heard from him." Moynihan steepled his fingers and pressed them against his lips. After a moment, he remarked, "I want you to gather together all of the clothes that you were wearing that night, outer garments as well as underwear, and pack them in a box. I will send an officer over to your parents' house to pick it up."

"Why on earth would you want my clothes?"

"It's a preemptive measure. It will rule out any gunshot residue and at the same time establish that any traces of blood that might be found are attributed to you and not your husband."

Lorraine looked away pensively. She would go to her parents' house and look for the garments she had worn on the night in question. Had she been in her yellow-and-white waitress uniform? Had she changed into casual attire? What shoes had she had on? These were the questions that came to mind. It was curious—she could remember everything else about that night, so how could she possibly not recall this?

·   ·   ·

Hours passed after Moynihan rejoined his team, collecting and labeling evidence. Lorraine busied herself in the kitchen, seemingly oblivious to the activity around her. Moynihan was observing the carpet being closely scrutinized and a clean, sharp putty knife being used to scrape flakes of several dry, stained fibers into a paper packet, when the second detective entered the room.

"I found this tucked away on a beam behind the heating unit in the cellar." It was a .22 caliber, nickel-plated, five-shot revolver. U.S. REVOLVER CO. and MADE IN USA were stamped on the top of the barrel.

Moynihan carefully examined the weapon and determined that three rounds remained in the cylinder. He removed the ammunition, placing it in a separate envelope, before securing the gun for transport to the crime lab. After the packaging was complete, he sat for a minute, deep in thought, before looking up at his colleagues.

"We know for a fact that the victim was shot twice in the head. One slug was retrieved during the autopsy. Forensics suggests that a second bullet exited the upper neck near the base of the skull. Let's cover every inch of this building and see if we can't find the errant missile."

It was dusk and the rain had relented by the time the team wrapped up their inspection. The stray bullet had gone undiscovered, despite a painstakingly thorough examination of the cottage. The shop, on the other hand, had revealed a large spool of 20gauge primary wire, the kind you could buy at any electrical-supply store. Moynihan absently added it to the collection of items destined for the state crime lab in Lawrence, before Lorraine reappeared.

"You've had a long day, Mr. Moynihan. I hope all the hard work contributes to something that will bring this awful affair to a close."

"I don't know if anything we uncovered today will solve this case, but at least we will take some consolation in knowing we did our job. We appreciate your cooperation." Moynihan waved his hat and headed for the door, before slowly coming to a stop and pivoting. "You know, there *is* one thing that struck me as odd. Your living room—it's nicely appointed, but it seems awfully spartan for someone who has lived here as long as you and Al have. I mean, no offense, but I really like a big, comfortable sofa to relax in when I get home."

"Well, of course you do, and so did my Al. When I closed the cottage, I moved his upholstered chair and ottoman to my parents' house, along with several other pieces of furniture."

"Ah, that explains it. Good night, Lorraine."

Outside, Moynihan climbed into the patrol car. "When we get back to the station, call the DA and tell him I need another search warrant, this one for Tom and Mary Janvrin's house on Maple Street."

.   .   .

Several days had passed when Nick received word that the district attorney's office had scheduled a press conference, to be held at two o'clock, regarding the Parker investigation. Newspaper journalists from as far as Boston were alerted. Things were moving quickly—just a day earlier, the body of Alvin Parker, Jr., had been interred at Mount Prospect Cemetery, with little fanfare. Now Nick was learning from Jade that full military services were to be observed later that morning at the Union Congregational Church.

"Who arranged for that?"

"Mr. and Mrs. Parker and, from what I'm hearing, the grieving widow will not attend, even though the Janvrins will be there with the three children."

"It doesn't sound like the Parkers and the Janvrins are maintaining anything resembling a unified front.

Are these typical in-law tensions, or do you think something more is going on here?"

"My instincts tell me there's no love lost. There was certainly some strain after she filed for divorce, but I think it was always a troubled relationship. Mothers-in-law usually get the bad rap, but in this case I have the sense that Lorraine was the great saboteur. The kids spent most of their time with the Janvrins; according to Mr. Parker, whenever they made plans to be with their grandchildren, Lorraine would show up late or call at the last minute to cancel because of something that had just 'popped up.' And she perfected the disappearing act. When they would arrive for a visit, she would retreat to another room to work on some project, or suddenly run out on an errand."

"A passive-aggressive personality if ever there was one. Why don't you pay your respects at the memorial service and see what more you can learn? I'm going to start working on my byline so that I can fill in the blanks after I hear what the DA has to say."

Chapter 4

THE ARREST

Nick drove to the district attorney's office and arrived just in time to find a seat close to the podium. A photographer from the *Boston American* recognized him from their days at the AP and came over to chat.

"Hello, Nick. Fancy meeting you here."

"Jack Smiley. It's always good to see you. They must have demoted you to the 'Town and Country' section."

"This is looking like a big story for our readers, Nick; my sources tell me the DA is about to name a suspect in the murder, and if that person turns out to be five foot two with eyes of blue, you can bet we'll be covering the case with two-inch headlines."

Although the comment caught Nick by surprise, he was about to play along, when the district attorney entered, along with a small entourage of officials. Logan Hughes had been a career prosecutor for ten years before he'd been elected as Essex County's district attorney. Tall and athletic, with a rectangular face and sturdy jawline, he was reputed to have been one of the finest tight ends ever to play football at Holy Cross. Nick had encountered him on numerous occasions but didn't know much more about him, other than that he seemed competent and ambitious. There was no amplification system, but Hughes had one of those powerful voices that carried across a room, so he asked for order.

"Ladies and gentlemen, thank you for attending this hastily assembled news conference. I have with me today Amesbury Police Chief Edmund Moynihan and State Police Lieutenant Frank Rizzo. Both of these gentlemen and their law enforcement agencies have been tremendous assets in assisting the district attorney's office in this investigation and in the collection of evidence in the murder of Alvin Parker, Jr., whose badly decomposed body was discovered last June in Merrimack River tidal waters. As a result of forensic evidence observed and recorded by the medical examiner's office, and physical evidence collected in the field by state and local investigators, an arrest warrant has now been issued for the detention and further interrogation of Lorraine Parker in connection with the disappearance and death of her late husband. Mrs. Parker will not be charged with a specific criminal complaint until she has had an opportunity to confer with legal counsel. A probable-cause hearing will be held at an early date to determine whether there is enough evidence to go to trial. I will now take questions."

The room was abuzz with a dozen or so newspaper reporters and at least one Boston television news broadcaster all shouting out questions at once. Hughes looked on impatiently, until he spied Nick and pointed at him, as if to acknowledge his seniority among the gaggle: "Mr. Ridgeway."

"District Attorney Hughes, what evidence has the prosecution collected, and how has the examination of this evidence prompted the arrest of Lorraine Parker as the lead suspect in the case?"

"There was no single piece of evidence that led us to suspect Mrs. Parker as a participant in this crime; rather, a preponderance of circumstantial evidence evolved that we felt required further explanation from the respondent. To give you one example: traces of human blood were found on the walls and carpet in the cottage at Lake Attitash. There was an apparent attempt to wash clean the spots, but bloodstains are stubborn and not easily expunged, even after the passage of time."

"It seems like there might be an acceptable explanation if, let's say, Alvin Parker injured himself in his own home, causing blood to stain areas of the room."

"A reasonable question, Mr. Ridgeway, but the bloodstain patterns we found suggest a forceful impact that caused the blood to break into smaller droplets, which then splattered on the wall in a pattern compatible with that produced by gunfire. At the same time, castoff stains, which produce an entirely different pattern, such as an open wound dragged across a surface might create, were also observed on the carpet. Neither of these stains is consistent with usual household accidents."

Smiley was quick with a follow-up question: "What about clothing? Surely the assailant's clothes would have to display some trace of the victim's blood."

"We confiscated several articles of clothing from Lorraine Parker, some of which were pieces she said she was wearing the night of her husband's disappearance."

"What exactly was seized?" Hughes paused to reclaim his eyeglasses from his breast pocket, balancing them at the end of his nose before reading from his legal pad.

"The articles taken were three pairs of shoes, including a pair of white waitress shoes, a pair of cloth slippers, and a pair of gold mesh sandals; a leopard-print brassiere; and a pair of beige cotton culottes with a broken zipper. I can tell you that so far our laboratory tests on these items have not yet resulted in any material criminal evidence. Nevertheless, yesterday a sheet, a pillowcase, and a hairbrush were found by a Merrimac police officer near the banks of the river on the route Mrs. Parker would have taken on her way to work the day after her husband was murdered. Copious human bloodstains were present on both the sheet and the pillowcase. The patrolman also found remnants from a newspaper dated April 9 next to the discarded articles."

"What about a murder weapon?" came a shout from the back of the room.

"Several firearms belonging to the victim were removed from the cottage, including a twenty-two caliber handgun, which some have speculated was the lethal weapon. As a result of tests conducted at the state police laboratory, we have disqualified it and are still looking for a murder weapon."

"Disqualified it—why?" Nick asked.

"During our investigation, we learned that several pieces of furniture had been removed to the home of Lorraine Parker's parents, Tom and Mary Janvrin. As a result, we obtained a search warrant and, upon examination of the furniture in question, discovered a bullet lodged in the frame between the seams of an overstuffed chair that had been taken from the cottage. When we compared that bullet to one fired from the twenty-two that we found in the cottage, the striations that are distinguished by the rifling of a barrel were not a match."

"But you did determine that the murder weapon, wherever it might be, was the one discharged in the cottage on the night in question."

"I will leave it you journalists to draw such conclusions, Mr. Ridgeway."

"The last time I checked, both motive and opportunity are necessary to prove a crime, Mr. Hughes. You seem to have established opportunity, but what about motive?"

Hughes took off his glasses and hesitated before responding. "At this point in time, we are not predisposed to discuss motive, Mr. Ridgeway."

.   .   .

Widow Held for Questioning in Parker Slaying

The *Daily News* headline and the story that followed ignited local chatter like a fast-spreading brushfire, as intense public interest fanned the flames. Whispers circulated of wild parties at the lake, racketeers peddling illicit drugs, adultery, and a police conspiracy to cover up the facts. By midweek Nick had received enough "tips" to fill a scandal sheet. Most were outlandish, but a few were credible enough that they required some measure of follow-up—for example, the small manila envelope that arrived in the mailroom. At first glance, it was just another letter addressed plainly to the *Daily News*. The letter, signed "Ten Wives" and postmarked Malden, Massachusetts, was a carbon copy of a missive neatly typed and addressed to Chief Edmund "Red" Moynihan.

> *Dear Sir:*
>
> *We are writing to you in the hope of obtaining the highest privilege of confidentiality. Your reputation as a law enforcement official of exceptional character and community virtue persuaded us to reach out in a desperate*

plea for discretion. We refer to a case that indirectly implicates certain members of the Lake Attitash community, whose reputations will be harshly impaired if gratuitous rumors are given credence through unsubstantiated testimony before a grand jury. We implore you to protect our children from the shame that will follow them if tales of wild parties and scandalous behavior are permitted to penetrate the walls—as they inevitably do—of an otherwise closed-door courtroom. Your investigations and interrogations of persons involved in this case notwithstanding, the lives and reputations of blameless individuals are at stake should careless testimony be allowed and later revealed. Please, sir, keep it out of the air.

Jade's eyes grew fixed, yet her expression betrayed no sign of surprise as she examined the letter Nick handed to her without explanation. When she finished, her mouth curved slightly into a half smile. "Sounds like there's more scandal and shame going on in Amesbury than I realized. How did you come upon this?"

"It arrived anonymously, and as the writer displays little admiration for the fourth estate, I have to assume that whoever sent this came by it somewhat furtively, hoping to use it to create a firestorm of drama and maybe break the case wide open. Since we're the people's watchdog, I suppose it deserves a little investigative reporting. Don't you agree?"

Jade gave him a knowing look, and her Mona Lisa smile reappeared as she grabbed her coat and headed for the door.

.   .   .

In downtown Newburyport, Fowles was the one place where you could grab the *Daily News* from the newsstand, read the sports page, and return it without paying a nickel; plus, it was a reasonable walk from the run-down apartment Artie Flynn occupied on Washington Street.

Artie sat in silence, coffee mug in one hand, newspaper in the other. The headline drew his eyes to the story he had known would land on the front page sooner or later. His relationship with Lorraine had been star-crossed from the beginning, and now this—it was a damn mess. Al Parker had been his pal, a guy you could talk to when you were restless and trying to push life in a new direction. That was the way it had been the first time Al had taken him to the cottage at Lake Attitash. Artie had been married for barely a year; his wife had kicked him out after she'd caught him fooling around with some lovestruck teenage girl he'd met at Hampton Beach. No matter who was to blame, the separation had been a blow to his self-esteem and had left him moody and disconsolate. That was when he'd met Lorraine. She was beautiful, yet she possessed simplicity—a purity to her personality—which she shared willingly, as if he were some stray mongrel that needed her attention. One smile from Lorraine was enough to massage any bruises his errant past had inflicted.

Pretty soon, he was a regular guest at the cottage, the gregarious social companion, and a forbidden temptation in Lorraine's otherwise dreary existence. So it seemed like a natural path when playful glances turned into ardent kissing while the kids were staying with her parents and Al was working the night shift at Hytron. In committing her first act of adultery, Lorraine had rationalized the affair as the awakening of a waning libido. Al had attended to her needs in an unsatisfactory manner, and now she had taken a lover to her bedroom, in an act not of selfishness but of emotional resuscitation.

To Artie, it was more complicated. He had never thought he could care about someone this much, but Lorraine was different. She was a seemingly delicate and innocent femme fatale who could lead you into compromising, even dangerous situations.

As he contemplated all that had happened in the year, he became aware of two figures standing over him. They wore gray fedoras that clearly identified them as cops, and the looks on their faces indicated they had some business to conduct.

"Arthur Flynn?" the taller one demanded. Artie gave no response, but the detective continued anyway. "We're picking you up for questioning. Our friends at the Amesbury Police Department would like a word with you. You can come voluntarily, or we can do it the hard way."

Artie raised his hands in a gesture of compliance. "Whatever you boys say."

"Let's go, wise guy."

Artie climbed into the backseat of an unmarked patrol car, with the second detective at his side. They drove across town and over the old Chain Bridge, which had connected Newburyport and Amesbury for more than a hundred years, before Red Moynihan and a uniformed officer met them.

The ride to the police station was brief, and Moynihan spoke hardly a word until they arrived. The squad room was busy with cops coming and going, none giving any notice to the civilian with the long black hair, combed back with a heavy dose of pomade. Average height, maybe a little shorter, with a toned build, he was what the Harps called black Irish.

Moynihan led him to a small, windowless room with a solitary table and two steel chairs. "Take a seat, Mr. Flynn, while I look over your file." His arrest history was brief: a couple of bar fights that caused some property damage but no personal injury; the usual traffic violations; public intoxication; and disorderly conduct. Moynihan was unmoved until the last entry caught his eye: "Morals charge—investigation pending." He sat down across from Artie, then crossed his legs while he read the remainder of the report. When he finished, he said nothing but drummed the fingers of his right hand on the table while quietly observing his antagonist. About a minute passed before Artie broke the ice: "What!"

Moynihan remained impassive, then poured a glass of water from a pitcher and gently slid it across the table.

"I didn't ask for water."

Moynihan looked down at the file once more, then said, "So, Arthur Flynn, tell me what you do for a living."

"I'm between jobs. What's it to you?"

"I'm just curious because it sounds like you're quite a Casanova."

"Too many ladies, too little time."

"Does that include married women?"

"I don't always ask, but sometimes the buzz goes out of a marriage, and if I can fill the void . . . it's probably some of the best sex they ever had."

"It says here that you've been named as a correspondent in a divorce case in Salem. How did that little slip-up happen?"

Artie squeezed his eyes shut and shook his head from side to side. "So, I'm paying an afternoon visit to this rich bitch I met at the casino about a month earlier. I'm just there for a little dick and dash when her husband shows up and makes a big scene. Seems he hired a private eye because he suspected his wife was sleeping around, and I'm the sucker who got caught with his pants down."

"Do you hang out at the casino often?"

Artie shrugged his shoulders. "It's a place to go when you're lookin' for a little action."

"Your record says that you were involved in a disturbance there last summer. Why don't you tell me about it?"

Artie looked warily at his interrogator. "It was a Friday night. The place was crowded, very crowded—you had to wait in line to get in. There was music in the background, so I was eyeballing the dance floor when I spied Lorraine Parker across the room."

"How did you know Lorraine Parker?"

"You know the answer to that question or you wouldn't have picked me up."

"Humor me."

"I worked with her husband, Al, at Hytron for about a year. 'Nuff said."

"So then what happened?"

"So I wander over to find out what she's doin' there because I don't see no Al. I say, 'Hey, Lorraine,' but she doesn't answer right away, so I get in her face, and damn if she doesn't look right through me. She's glassy-eyed, like she's doped up or something, when this foreign dude, all tricked out, tells me to quit bothering the lady. I know something's not right, so I tell him to fuck off and he takes offense and tells me I'm out of line. So I explain to him, very politely, 'If you're lookin' for trouble, pal, you just found it.' Next thing I know, one of his goons sucker-punches me and I'm out on the street."

"It says here you caused some mayhem yourself."

"You bet your sweet ass. I start down the boardwalk, and who do I run into at the arcade but Owen Quinney and a couple of his townies. I tell him what happened, so we go back into the casino and beat the shit out of these amateurs. By the time I look around, Mr. Suave and Lorraine are out the door and climbing into his Poon Caddy. Next thing I know, the cops arrive and I'm cooked for the night."

Moynihan eyed him summarily before changing the subject. "How would you describe your relationship with Lorraine Parker?"

"We liked the same food. We'd go out to eat together."

"Would you say you had an intellectual relationship?"

"No, no, no."

"Would you say your relationship was one you would find appropriate to have with your best friend's wife?"

"Yeah, sure."

"Was she in love with you?"

"I don't know—maybe. Why don't you ask her?"

"Do you deny having intercourse with Lorraine Parker?"

"Yes."

"How many times after Al Parker disappeared did you see her?"

"Four or five."

"Did you go out with other girls during the time you were seeing Lorraine?"

"Look, what are you getting at?"

"Did she tell you she was in love with you, and can you tell me you had no interest in her?"

Artie flew off the handle. "Why can't we talk about Al? He's the wife beater, for Chrissake."

Moynihan paused and lit up a cigarette, then offered one to Artie.

"No, thanks. I don't smoke."

"I've got one more question for you, Artie; then I'm going to let you go. Do you own a gun?"

"No, I don't own no guns. What do I need a gun for?"

"I hear you've done a little collection work—seems like a gun might give you some extra power of persuasion."

"Are you kidding? You pull a gun on somebody, they're not gonna forget it, and maybe they might kill your ass next time you come around. No, I don't pack no heat."

"What about Al. Did Al own any guns?"

"Sure. Al used to hunt, so he had guns."

"Any pistols?"

"Yeah, he had a couple. We used to shoot squirrels up at the lake."

"So, you're saying he owned two pistols."

"Yeah, as far as I know, he owned two pistols."

Chapter 5

THE CLIQUE

A mesbury was a quintessential New England town, just distant enough from Boston and unwanted affectations to keep everyday life reasonably simple, as it had been for one generation after another. Where Newburyport boasted elegant mansions and the nickname Clipper City from its early days as a thriving seaport, a more diffident town existed on the opposite side of the Merrimack, one where textile mills, hat factories, and carriage shops had held sway before the Great Depression. Now local merchants, small manufacturers, boat builders, and friendly shopkeepers prospered modestly in a local economy that sustained a population of ten thousand residents of predominantly English, Irish, and French-Canadian descent. However, a restlessness pervaded the postwar social order, which seemed to cast aside the mores of the preceding generation. It was a malaise brought on not by greed or selfishness but by a careless need for enlightened indulgence, and even Amesbury's provincial borders could not dampen it.

The rumors had circulated for years. Although no names and no proof ever surfaced to give absolute credence to the stories of wild parties, lurid tales of wife swapping among a smart group of mostly young couples attempting to relieve the boredom of quotidian living in suburbia were whispered on the golf course, across card tables, or over idle coffee chatter. Numerous labels were assigned to the participants; some called them the Set, but those in the know came to refer to them as the Clique, and the name stuck.

Jade began calling a few acquaintances to see if she could dial into some of the conversation about the Clique. She wasn't an Amesbury girl by birth, but she knew enough of the chin-wags to get a line on who might be a reliable informant. Most had boundless gossip to share, but none of it revealed any firsthand knowledge, until an unlikely source gave her the lead she was seeking.

Sophie Gauthier owned and operated a laundry on Route 110, a busy stretch of roadway that led to Merrimac and Haverhill. Jade patronized the place and was picking up her own laundry, as Sophie had a convenient wash, dry, and fold service. Sophie was an inveterate talker, and today she was complaining about the bed linens that one of her customers dropped off with enough regularity to arouse Sophie's suspicions.

"I don't know what goes on up there, but I'm here to tell you, it's no good! These sheets come in here every other week soiled with all kinds of filth—you name it. And look at this—a rubber!" Sophie held out a clothespin to display a used condom. "It's Sodom and Gomorrah, I tell you."

"Where is 'up there'?" Jade asked, feigning shock.

"Up on the lake. They cavort there all year long. Up go the headlamps at night; down comes the bedding the next day. It's like a motel, I tell you."

Jade, having long ago mastered the art of reading upside down, glanced at the laundry slip: Patricia Martin.

.   .   .

Patty Martin was caught off guard by a knock on the door of her tidy home in Newburyport, where she and her husband, Mike, a contractor, had once led a quiet, respectable, perhaps dull, but satisfying life. She was a member of the garden club and the Junior League, with a priggish outlook on the world around her.

That lifestyle had changed after they bought the cottage on Lake Attitash, an idyllic getaway where they could escape the hot, dry weather that arrived every July and remained off and on until after Labor Day. A tranquil pond with swimming beaches along the shoreline, Attitash was large enough to accommodate small recreational boats for fishing and sailing.

Soon after Patty and Mike moved in to this seasonal retreat, they were invited to join a small congenial group of married couples, most in their thirties, who had a mutual partiality for stylish dress and a well-shaken cocktail. Patty was petite and had kept her schoolgirl figure, while Mike remained fit through everyday labor, so it did not take long for certain members of the group to target them for a more intimate contest of flattery and indulgence. The game was simple enough: the men threw their keys into a salad bowl, and the wives reached in at random to determine who would be their partner for an evening of blissful pleasure. The men could talk about whatever they wanted, but the ladies made the rules. This arrangement created a level of excitement that Patty and Mike had never experienced in their otherwise happy, monogamous marriage. An impersonal way to have sex—why, it was almost like dancing with another woman's husband. What might have seemed scandalous a year earlier had become a gratifying, even vital piece of their matrimonial existence.

"I won't even ask how you found me, Miss Lash," Patty said aimlessly, after learning the reason for Jade's visit, "but I have dreaded this moment ever since the Parker case hit the newspapers. I'll tell you whatever you want to know, but please, I beg you, keep my name out of it."

"I promise you that whatever you reveal to me will be attributed to an anonymous source. Now, why don't you just start at the beginning?"

Patty filled her in on their seductive entrée into the Clique, providing enough salacious details of sexual transgressions to fill a gossip column, before Jade redirected the conversation toward its membership. "What can you tell me about the other participants?"

"They're mostly ordinary people—doctors, lawyers, businessmen, and their wives. There are one or two who I'm pretty sure are prominent, but they keep a low profile. Of course, you don't have to be married to be in the mix, but you aren't allowed to fly solo."

"Are they all from around here?"

"Most are, of course, but a few are from the artist colony in Rockport, and there's one couple who regularly make the trip from Boston. Then there's the Baron. Some people say he's descended from a line of Hungarian aristocrats, but I have my doubts. I don't know his last name, but he introduces himself as Andros. He's certainly mysterious, arriving in a big black limousine and departing with hardly a goodbye."

"Whom does he arrive with?"

"I never could figure that out. The only female I ever saw him with during the cocktail hour was Lorraine Parker, and since I didn't know Alvin from Adam, it's possible that she and the Baron arrived as a couple, but I can't swear to it."

"When did Lorraine join the group?"

"The first time I ever laid eyes on her was last fall. She attracted a lot of attention from the men, and that caused more than a little jealousy among some of the wives. We all knew why we were there—to sleep with someone else's husband—but woe to anyone whose sexual attraction threatened to upset the balance of trade, so to speak."

"But you were pairing up as a matter of chance, weren't you? By the luck of the draw."

"Perhaps, but when you're part of the body gallery, the feline claws tend to reveal themselves when someone prettier walks into the room. Lorraine drew a lot of snide remarks about her plain wardrobe; some people became downright snooty, as though she and Al were nothing more than poor relations."

"So, Al was there?"

"Like I said, I couldn't pick him out of a lineup if my life depended on it. Their house is at the opposite end of the lake, I don't recall ever meeting him, and I certainly never slept with him."

"Explain to me how this all worked. You served cocktails and socialized for an hour or so, before the men tossed their keys into a hat, and then what?"

"Then the ladies reached in and each one selected her partner for the evening. Usually the fellow drove his 'date' to her house for a two-hour 'encounter,' as we like to call it, before returning to the lair. A few, especially the long-distance guests, either found a spare bedroom or opted for a motel room in Salisbury."

"And did everyone always return to the 'lair,' as you put it?"

"Most did, because that was how they would re-unite with their mate. Some would even stay and have a nightcap before heading home."

"How about Lorraine?"

"No, I never saw Lorraine at the end of an evening. I just assumed that she remained at her cottage, since it was only a couple of miles away."

"And when was the last time you saw Lorraine?"

Patty cast her gaze downward, before looking back up at Jade. "The weekend before Alvin Parker's disappearance."

.   .   .

Nick did some digging and traced to a limousine company in East Boston the black Cadillac that both Eddie Cook and Patty Martin had described. After a little friendly persuasion and a couple of sawbucks, he learned that the vehicle was leased to the Canadian consulate general in Boston's Back Bay. Nick called Information, then dialed the number he had requested.

"Canadian consulate. How may I direct your call?"

"I'd like to speak to Andros."

"Excuse me, sir—what is the person's last name?"

"Andros is the only name I have. It is imperative that I speak with him."

"I am sorry, sir. I cannot connect you if you do not know his surname."

"Dammit, I do not have the gentleman's last name, but he implored me to contact him and said that should I telephone, I would be directed to his office without hesitation. I insist that you connect me at once. It's a matter of great importance."

Silence was followed by a terse response. "Andros Farkas, the attaché for the Hungarian diaspora, has departed for Montreal. He left no forwarding address."

"Yes, thank you. I will attempt to contact him there."

.   .   .

Andy Durgin was a distant cousin through Nick's mother's side of the family, but they were also childhood chums and kept in touch when they could, which usually meant at weddings and funerals. Andy was a retired naval intelligence officer who maintained a long list of State Department contacts, as well as a network of moles that he had once used to help Nick in another investigation.

Nick placed a call to Andy from the city desk and after the usual pleasantries got down to business. "My investigation keeps leading me back to this Baron, Andros Farkas, who is allegedly a Hungarian national. I tracked him to the Canadian consulate in Boston, and from what I can tell, he has some level of diplomatic authority, but I don't have a good feeling about him, Andy, I think he's up to some sort of mischief."

"Well, at least his cover adds up; ever since the Soviet occupation, Hungarian refugees have been fleeing to the US and Canada by way of Austria. This diaspora consists of displaced Hungarians living in Canada. What else can you tell me about Farkas?"

"Not a lot more. He's about fifty, average weight and height, dresses flamboyantly, and has a penchant for attractive younger females. He occasionally travels with several part-time bodyguards."

"Give me a couple of days, and I'll see what I can find out. If this guy's legitimate, we should be able to pick up some kind of diplomatic trail in the foreign office."

.   .   .

Andros Farkas boarded the *Maple Leaf Express*, making his way to the familiar compartment for the eight-hour train ride to Montreal. The porter acknowledged his presence and without prompting delivered a Chivas and soda.

Andros was not descended from the legitimate male lineage of dynastic families; rather, he was the product of what was called a left-hand marriage. His father, a titled aristocrat of middle-ranked nobility, had married a commoner, thereby denying his children any claim to succession rights. But Andros had a ruthless determination to climb the rugged ladder of society, as an arriviste if not dynastically. An émigré to Montreal, he began his rise by bootlegging Canadian whiskey across the border to the United States, avoiding costly excise taxes and selling it to dishonest distributors up and down the Atlantic seaboard. It was a lucrative enterprise and introduced him to the business of high-end escort services, which he exported to the United States by enticing pretty Québecois girls to leave the streets of Montreal for the safer boardwalks of Ogunquit, Old Orchard, and Hampton Beach, where he could control the low-key action without interference from the gangs of Ville-Marie. As a Hungarian expatriate attached to the Canadian consulate, he had unrestricted access to and from the United States and used the position to supply the summer enclaves of New England with young ladies who could hold a conversation at a dinner party as well as anything else. It was with one of these ingénues that he penetrated the clandestine affairs of the Clique. An acquaintance from Boston was a regular participant and arranged for his introduction, which he attended to with mild curiosity. While his escort was popular among the men for her skill and social dexterity, the natural beauty, lack of vanity, and unaffected manners of one of the other guests beguiled Andros.

He flattered the object of his infatuation with a regal persona that she found equally appealing, in spite of the fact that he could easily have been mistaken for her father, given their difference in age. So, through a sleight of hand aided by a hastily conducted business exchange with the master of the house, Andros made certain that the keys to the Cadillac were presented to Lorraine Parker as her draw from the selection pool.

Chapter 6
SWEET LORRAINE

Red Moynihan pressed his knuckles to his chin, fingers interlocked, as he looked across the desk at Logan Hughes. The DA knew that the evidence collected was circumstantial, yet both men realized they had little choice but to charge Lorraine Parker with murder. The case was gaining national attention, in part because of the rumors about wild parties and carnal escapades, but also because Lorraine simply didn't fit the profile of a murderess. She was young and pretty, the demure mother of three children, and seemed blithely incapable of such a dastardly act. And her demeanor evoked purity, as though the events of the last ten days were nothing more than a big misunderstanding. Moynihan deigned to believe her, and he wanted more than anything to find the missing clue that would cast suspicion in a different direction. But the evidence, circumstantial as it might be, was weighty. Even now, the state police crime lab confirmed that traces of blood two months old had been discovered on the Rocks

Village Bridge. Alvin Parker's Navy records revealed that he was B positive, the third most common blood type, though at 9 percent it was a statistical minority compared with A- and O-type donors. Hughes read aloud the report confirming that the blood found on the bridge was type B.

"So, Al Parker was type B—so are twenty million other people," Moynihan mused.

"Yeah, but those other twenty million people didn't wind up in the bottom of the Merrimack."

"Okay, so here's what's bothering me. Lorraine weighs what—a hundred and fifteen pounds? How does a woman that size lift a dead man's body, trussed with weights, over a four-foot rail on the Rocks Village Bridge?"

"Clearly, she had an accomplice, and she needs to name him now if she wants to avoid the death penalty."

"The death penalty?"

"That's what the public will demand if this goes to trial."

"Logan, we're talking about Lorraine Parker, not Lizzie Borden. I've known the Janvrins since she was in grade school. They're good people."

"Good people can produce bad offspring, Red, and sometimes a bad seed can remain dormant until it awakens inexplicably, in this case propelling Lorraine Parker into reckless proclivities and an uncontainable desire to possess what she wanted at all cost."

"Like what?"

"Well, that's the mystery, isn't it? That's precisely what Nick Ridgeway demanded of me at the press conference—a motive. You're going to have to work hard on her, Red. Find out what was deep inside her mind, what drove Lorraine Parker to murder her husband, and who it was that helped her dispose of the body. We need to pursue indictments at all cost."

"I'll do it, Logan, I'll do it at your direction, but without pride or principle. I've been in law enforcement all my life, and I cannot presume guilt or innocence, nor will I coerce Lorraine Parker into a confession just to disguise your refusal to prosecute this case under usual criminal procedures." Hughes looked at him stoically.

"Just do your job."

.   .   .

Within the borders of Amesbury, an alliance had been formed from the ranks of respected citizens to support the police in finding a solution to the murder and pursuing every lead. It was sought as a way to defuse the scandal that had overspread the town, while holding an insatiable press at bay. Even the mayor got in on the act, telling newspapers that a solution was essential to repair Amesbury's reputation. The tips led Moynihan to dozens of interviews, including with persons residing in the vicinity of Rocks Village, who told him that on the night in question, they heard men's loud voices arguing, then two loud shots interspersed with what sounded like a woman's screams. He filed a report, but nothing ever came of it. Later he sent a diver, a former Navy frogman, to scour the river bottom beneath the bridge, where he salvaged an old iron radiator, a tire wheel, and even a gun, which proved to be of no interest in the investigation. He interviewed the doctor who had been called on to treat Lorraine after she claimed to have received a beating from Al on the night of his disappearance; he stated that the marks consisted of nothing more than a superficial bruise and a slight scratch on her chin.

By the end of the week, he felt like he was back to square one, with no new credible information and no progress, when he got a call from an unlikely informant. Nick Ridgeway wanted to meet to talk with him about a new element in the case—something that could lead the investigation in a new direction. The information was not privileged, but he wanted to share it with Moynihan to avoid any misconceptions that he had withheld evidence from the authorities.

They met for coffee at White's Lunch, not far from town hall, neutral ground for cops and newshounds.

"You guys in the press corps haven't made it any easier for us. Every time you print a new allegation, the switchboard lights up with callers, mostly from the self-styled virtuous crowd, demanding that we conduct raids on the lake to force the sinners to cease and repent."

"It's a big story, Red, and if we don't cover every angle, the tabloids will control the narrative and you won't be too happy with the results."

"I know. As the saying goes, 'Better the devil you know . . .' So, what have you got for me?"

"I've got a mystery man, a Pygmalion of sorts, whose fervent pursuit of Lorraine Parker may have been transformative, to the point where she surrendered control of her moral compass. He plays the role of a power broker with international connections, but when you boil it all down, I suspect he's nothing more than a bootlegger and a pimp. His name is Andros Farkas; he's a Hungarian national."

"I heard about this character—they call him the Baron. I questioned Lorraine about him, but she denies knowing him, and whenever I tried to follow a trail, it went cold, like he never existed—one dead end after another."

"Oh, he exists, all right, but he's fled to Canada, where you can't extradite him even if you can tie him to the murder. He's the official attaché to the Hungarian diaspora and as such is entitled to diplomatic immunity."

"How do you know all this?"

"Let's just say I have a contact who specializes in these kinds of investigations."

"So, what's his influence over Lorraine, and how does he figure into the murder?"

"Lorraine was introduced to him through the Lake Attitash crowd, the one everyone calls the Clique. Farkas had apparently become bored with the girls in his employ; they were prostitutes, and he longed for more of a relationship. He was captivated by Lorraine's naiveté and charm, and as the courtship expanded outside the group, Farkas became everything she could ever imagine. He was a highflier and charismatic—a dark prince, so to speak—and as a result, I think she changed into something alien, a femme fatale desperate to find and rescue herself from her bleak, unhappy marriage at any cost."

"So, you think she murdered Al Parker to be with this Baron von Farkas?"

"It's all hearsay, but he claims she shot Parker twice in the head, then called him to clean up the mess." Moynihan let the words sink in. The whole idea made him uneasy, as though Hollywood had taken over his little corner of the world in order to conjure up some film noir full of pessimism, fatalism, and menace. His body asserted itself, his palms pressing down on the table, as he stood up and put on his hat to leave.

"Don't write your story just yet, Nick. Let me follow up on a couple of leads. I'll get back to you."

"To be continued," Nick replied, "and under wraps for now."

.   .   .

The house on Wharf Road was compact but idyllic, with a view of the Atlantic and a small but carefully tended garden. As the crow flies, Rockport was only about twenty miles away, but navigating the highways and byways to the tip of Cape Ann lengthened the route to thirty-five miles and a good hour's drive.

The homeowner, Marie Leveque, was a faintly stout woman in her midthirties, dressed casually if somewhat daringly in a low-cut blouse and wearing the baubles and beads that she designed and sold at one of the artist shops out on the Neck. Her husband, a chiropractor with a successful practice in Gloucester, had bought the place as a present to consummate their remarriages, the second time around for both. Jade had persuaded Patty Martin to reveal the identity of one of the Clique's out-of-towners, somebody less likely to be worried about the local gossip or the ignominy that could shadow them around Amesbury, and the effusive Marie was content to talk so long as her picture would not appear in the paper.

"So, Patty Martin gave me up? Oh, that's rich," she said, with a sardonic laugh. "I'll tell you something: that broad always acted like she was better than everyone else in the room, and judgmental—very, very judgmental. I mean, she had the nerve to comment on my perfume when I was getting all dolled up for the rapport, as I like to call it. Can you imagine—that tight-assed Junior Leaguer telling me what fragrance I should or should not wear?"

"It sounds like you had a pretty diverse group of partygoers. I mean, there must have been some who were kinder than others."

"Oh, sure, we had our favorites, especially this one couple—I called them Fred and Ginger because they were marvelous dancers. I'd cut in every so often, and Fred would just sweep me off my feet."

"And how about the Parkers?"

"Well, I figured you didn't come all the way out here to talk about my flair for ballroom dancing, did you? Yes, the Parkers—there's a sad story, and one that I can't figure out. She was just as sweet and polite as they come, and as pretty as a daisy. I think most of the men had an eye for her, but she kept her distance; she didn't socialize very much during the cocktail hour. I told Harry—that's my husband—I told Harry it was a good thing he never got switched up with that sweet Lorraine, or he might be sleeping with the sturgeon." She tittered.

"What was your impression of Al Parker?"

"I was impressed at first, but then I came to think that the fella I thought was Al Parker wasn't Al Parker after all."

"Really? Was it by any chance a gentleman they called the Baron?"

"Oh, gosh, no—we all knew Andros. He was no man of mystery around here. He even visited my shop on one occasion and bought some jewelry for his girls—and he arrived on the scene much later."

"So, whom did you mistake for Al Parker?"

"Well, I don't really know. He was a tall, strapping fellow; he looked very athletic and was a sharp dresser—I remember he wore a very pretty purple tie."

"So, you really don't know if you ever met Al Parker."

"Well, now that you mention it, I guess not."

"Back to Mr. Tall, Dark, and Handsome—I take it he wasn't a regular."

"No, but I guarantee you I've seen his face before, outside of the Clique. I just can't remember where or when."

"Do you recall who else he hooked up with?"

"No, once you drew your partner, you were pretty focused on your date and everything else was a blur."

"But if you mistook him for Al Parker, he must have been with Lorraine on at least one occasion, no?"

"Oh, absolutely. Whenever he was front and center, she was glued to his side."

.   .   .

Lorraine's friends later wondered how she had fallen in with such a crowd. It began on one of those unpredictably mild spring evenings as she walked the lakeshore while the kids were away and Al was at work. Most of the cottages were still buttoned down for the season, save a few whose occupants found the month of May a perfect time to unwind and awaken from hibernation the otherwise picturesque grounds. Lorraine was restless as she thought about the dalliance that had unsettled her marriage. It was not so much guilt that dogged her as a question of what next. Was she to go through life looking for something that didn't exist?

The sweet smell of balsam filled the air and was satisfying her senses, easing her troubled spirits, when the sudden baritone of a motorcar rumbled up next to her.

"Good evening, mademoiselle—I wonder if you can you direct me to this cottage?"

At first she didn't notice the driver so much as the car, a black Ford Crestline with red interior and gleaming whitewall tires. It was a new model, and the bright, polished finish mesmerized her for a moment before she looked up the man at the wheel, who regarded her with soft blue eyes and a smile. "It's not as though I'm lost—why, I've been to this lake a few times—but I have this invitation and no address."

Lorraine looked at the card. The sender had scribbled a crude map of Lake Attitash, with several homes and the narrow lanes that surrounded it, but it was nearly impossible to follow unless you lived there.

"I know where this is, but it's at the complete opposite end of the lake. The best thing would be for me to guide you there—it's a beautiful night, and I can walk home. Of course, you *are* a stranger, so . . ." Her voice trailed off, and she furrowed her brow in an exaggerated look of consternation.

"Well, hop in and I'll tell you all about myself while you direct me to my destination."

For some reason, she felt perfectly safe getting into the man's car, and the enjoyment of meeting someone new, someone who was not only outgoing but handsome, seemed a daring proposition.

The man began, "I was raised in Ohio, but I came east to attend college and I never left. I fell in love with the ocean and the seasons, and Ipswich seemed like an ideal place to settle down, but it was a little too slow and provincial. I've been divorced for about three years now, and Newburyport feels young and vibrant, so I bought a place out near Joppa Flats."

"My, you've told me more about yourself in thirty seconds that most men I know will reveal in a month. Take a left at the end of this road."

"I wasn't always so chatty, but my therapist tells me I need to be less restrained, so I push myself. That's why I'm going to this cocktail party tonight—to expand my social horizons, so to speak."

"Well, I guess we could all do with a little of that—next right and down the lane, to the third house on the right." From within came the sounds of loud music and laughter that seemed to echo across the lake. Lights illuminated every window, showing people moving about like fading silhouettes on a stage.

"Why don't you come in with me?" he asked.

"I'm not sure I would be welcome. I mean, *you're* the one with the invitation," she said.

"We're allowed to bring guests."

"I'll probably know some of the people here, at least by sight."

"Then you will have the advantage," the man said.

Chapter 7
DALTON HOUSE AND JAKE'S

Nick persuaded Jade to meet at the Dalton Club in Newburyport for a late afternoon aperitif and debriefing. Dalton House was one of those traditional gentlemen's saloons that allowed ladies entry only through a side door and only at certain times of the year—and today wasn't one of them. An eighteenth-century ship captain had built the home on State Street, and its walls had seen much history before it had been turned into a men's social club after the turn of the century. It was a ritual for bankers, lawyers, and even newspapermen to frequent the men's bar at sunset for cocktails, oysters on the half shell, and a good cigar.

Jade arrived just moments before a waiter emerged with a Tom Collins and a Manhattan, straight up. She sipped the citrusy mixture and peered suspiciously through the cigar smoke at the patrons, with their three-piece suits, manicured nails, and closely cropped hair.

"Aren't you afraid they'll blackball you for bringing your catholic, left-leaning girlfriend into this den of WASP-y prep school boys?"

"Nah, they know that we know where all the skeletons are hidden. Besides, see that fellow with the mustache over there? I'm told he's a Baptist. We've become very progressive." She laughed at the remark. Jade was slender yet arresting, a freckle-faced brunette who could still turn a few heads as she swept into a room. It was not so much her looks as a certain vitality that she radiated—it was the way she carried herself, he thought. Even here, in stodgy old Dalton House, on a day when the distaff were not welcome, Nick could sense, with sufficient redress at his heedless indiscretion, the furtive glances from the proper old Yankees scattered across the room. "So, what new information do you have for our readers?"

"Well, it's the same old tale, but with a new twist. It seems there might be another man in Lorraine's life besides the Baron and Artie Flynn, a leading-man type who made a brief appearance in the Clique before exiting the stage."

"Bachelor number three, eh? From naive schoolgirl to man-eater?"

"I don't think so. She seems less predator and more hapless prey in this whole drama. There's no cast of spiteful, immoral people in a sex-secret town here. They might not get an A rating from the Catholic

League of Decency, but they meant no harm. They simply wanted to redefine their moral limits, and Lorraine got swept up in it. I think she was vulnerable and became somewhat reliant on number three."

"Women's intuition?"

"Call it what you will, but I will guarantee you this—emotionally, she was never on equal footing."

"What about Farkas?"

"The Baron was larger than life, a free-spending playboy, and someone to regard, but my instincts tell me she didn't love him. He was ephemeral, a passing fancy, and never in the running."

"And Artie Flynn?"

"I talked with Artie's estranged wife. They still see each other. He comes by whenever he feels spurned, and he definitely wears his heart on his sleeve. She acknowledges that Artie was a wandering gunslinger and Lorraine's paramour, but she claims it didn't take Lorraine long to outgrow his banality. The only time he made her happy was in the bedroom. Of course, he would do anything for her, but she was out of his league."

"Might that include the disappearance of the essential corpus delicti?"

"If you mean did he dispose of the body, it's not outside the realm of possibilities in this case."

"I sure would like to get a chance to have a conversation with the loquacious Arthur Flynn. What do you think the chances of that happening are?"

"I don't know. Moynihan has him on a short leash, and he won't take kindly to any obvious interference. Why don't you see if Eddie Cook can make that happen?"

.   .   .

Jake's Café on Merrimac Street wasn't really as much a café as it was a neighborhood bar with a pool table and a bad reputation. It had no particular decor and made no pretenses of style. It was one of those grimy enclaves where the regulars are there before you arrive and after you leave.

Artie Flynn responded to Nick's secondhand invitation to meet with a note scribbled on the back of a betting stub from Seabrook Greyhound Park: "Jake's, 8:00 Tuesday." The message was impaled on a note spindle on his desk, with no explanation from the newsroom staff for how it had gotten there. The barroom was smoky and dark, and Nick stood motionless for a few seconds, waiting for his eyes to adjust. A half dozen or more patrons were sitting at the bar, and one bartender, a woman in her fifties, poured drinks while another haggard, old woman made her way around the booths that encompassed the room.

Nick looked at his watch, thinking he was early, when he caught a glimpse of the neon Pabst Blue Ribbon sign glistening off the pomade of the dark, wavy hair of a solitary customer in the corner. He made his way slowly to the booth, as Artie Flynn looked him over.

"Hello, Artie. I'm Nick Ridgeway."

"I didn't think you were Father Flanagan."

Nick eased himself into the booth across from Flynn as the old waitress shuffled over. He figured a Manhattan wasn't a good idea, so he ordered a beer and one more for his host, who quickly added, "And a couple of those pickled eggs, Gladys."

"So, you're a regular here?"

"It's a place to hang out, and the drafts are a quarter—hard to beat."

"I've probably driven by this place a hundred times, and it's the first time I've stopped in."

Artie let out a sarcastic chuckle. "This ain't exactly the Dalton Club, Mr. Ridgeway."

"No, but it's so much more casual, and you can be seated right away, and, as you say, drafts are just a quarter."

Artie's smirk gradually transformed to a broad grin. "Eddie Cook says you're okay, so I guess you are."

Gladys brought the beers and wiped the table with a wet, dirty rag, before placing a bowl with the pickled eggs before them. Artie gestured at the barroom delicacy, but Nick declined with a polite wave of the hand. "Heh-heh-heh, that's why I ordered two—I figured you were an easy mark."

Despite the pungent aroma, Nick got down to business. "I'm pretty sure you know why I asked to meet with you, Artie."

"Sure. Like every other wise guy in town, you want to find out what I know about the Parker murder. Well, let me tell you something: I may not be an altar boy, but I'm no killer, either. You want to ask me how it happened? I can only tell you what I know, or maybe I should say what I *don't* know, but it's off the record, pal. Moynihan will use any excuse to send me up the river, and I'm not planning to do no time, capisce?"

"Let's start at the beginning. How long were you and Lorraine lovers?"

"It started in the summer. I wasn't looking for it—Al was my buddy—but something hit me like a thunderbolt, and she was pretty keen on it, too. I'd go over there when Al was at work, or she'd sneak over to my place during the day. It was a pretty good arrangement."

"So, what happened?"

"I'll tell you what happened. All of a sudden, she got in tight with this group up at the Lake, and before I knew it, I was like the odd man out with this bunch of oversexed amateurs. I asked her what was going on, but she iced me—she said she was taking her emotional self to a next level and started talking about yin and yang and her active positive forces. She was wacky, I tell you. Then, the next thing I know, she's hanging out with this Baron character, who I later find out is pimping broads from Ogunquit to Hampton Beach."

"So then what did you do?"

"There was nothin' I *could* do. She was totally infatuated with the little dickhead, until finally he stopped seeing her."

"How did you learn that he had stopped seeing her?"

"She told me. I decided to go over to see her one day, and she seemed like a new person. She was all smiles and happy, so I suggested maybe we should get back together, but she just said no, she was moving on to a new chapter in her life."

"So then what?"

"So then nothin'. She was just a sweet memory in my rearview mirror until she called about a month later. It was late, about eleven thirty, when the phone rang. She was bawling her eyes out and begged me to come over. I could tell something was very wrong, so I rode my Harley to the lake, fast as I could. When I got there, Al was slouched in his chair and I could see blood on his face, so I said, 'What happened here?' but Lorraine just stared at me like she was in a state of shock. That's when I saw the gun on the floor and realized he'd been shot. I thought, *I've got to get her outta here and figure out what the hell happened.*

"So I got her into Al's car and I drove her to my place. She was nervous but calm by the time we arrived, so I asked what had happened to Al and she said she'd shot him by accident. I said, 'If it was an accident, why don't we call the police?'

'No,' she said. 'I just want everything to go away, I want Al to go away, I want the Clique to go away, I just want my life back again, you have to help me do this. If I call the police, they'll arrest me, and I'll go on trial, and the whole world will know about this madness—all the lies, the adultery. I cannot permit the shame and humiliation that will surely follow my children.' She looked me in the eye with that look, that sweet Lorraine look, and I knew what I had to do." Artie finished his beer, and I asked if he wanted another. "Nah, one more won't make this stinkin' memory go away." Nick paused for a minute to let the words sink in.

"So, what *did* you do?"

"Here's where it gets interesting. We went back to the cottage—it was about three o'clock in the morning—and I grabbed a couple of cinder blocks and some electrical wire, and I started tying up the body, when I noticed something funny: there was a second bullet hole in Al's head, right by the temple. I was pretty sure it wasn't there three hours earlier, so I asked Lorraine how many times she shot him. She said once, in the face. I said that's what I thought. I didn't say anything more; I just finished the job and we put him in the trunk of the car, then cleaned up the mess. By the time we got to the Rocks Village Bridge, I could see the sun coming up in the east, so I dumped the body over the side close to West Newbury, where the shadows gave us more cover and I knew the water was deep."

"So, you think someone else came in and finished the job?"

"Like I said, I can't tell you what I don't know, but I do know this: when we got back to the cottage, the gun was gone. Man-o-man, I looked everywhere, but that friggin' heater was nowhere to be found."

·   ·   ·

The next day, Nick decided to drive to Lake Attitash to see with his own eyes the place where a complicated web of extramarital affairs had led to a loss of innocence, then betrayal, and ultimately murder. He exited the main thoroughfare, where graded dirt roads looped their way through one honeycomb after another of clustered, simple, lakefront cottages, until the homes became more solitary and distant from one another. The lake was sky blue and placid, as a bank of towering, dark clouds gathered in the southwest on the opposite end of the pond, even though the sun still shone overhead as he arrived at the cottage. Gardens decorated the front stoop on either side; once tidy with marigolds and zinnias, they were now overgrown and crowded by weeds. The door was unlocked, which was the norm during the summer season; after all, Attitash was a safe place where children came and went freely between the beaches and the homes of friends and neighbors. Inside the cottage was sparse, at least in the downstairs, where Al and Lorraine made the adjustment from high school sweethearts to husband and wife, raising a family of three kids born one after another during the cheerful years of marriage.

Nick looked in the kitchen. A porcelain sink showed streaks of green where water from an artesian well had left timeworn but enduring stains resulting from calcium and magnesium in the soil. Above was a small hand-painted sign that read: "Thankful, grateful, and truly blessed."

He ascended the stairs to the second floor, which was really a loft with gabled dormers. He sat on the end of a bed in a space obviously furnished for children. The walls were cluttered with homemade signs from summer games past, one announcing a children's masquerade, another proclaiming the rules and territory of a capture-the-flag night. He spied a book on the nightstand by Edgar Allan Poe, with a page that was carefully dog-eared, as if to bring the reader back to a favorite passage read and recited aloud a hundred times. Nick grasped the book, and it opened naturally to its intended poem.

In youth's spring it was my lot
To haunt, of the wide earth a spot
The which I could not love the less,
So lovely was the loneliness
Of a wild lake, with black rock bound,
And the tall pines that tower'd around.

As he slowly closed the book and carefully returned it to its former resting place, a sadness came over him. He had come here expecting to discover an empty house, a cold, bitter place where kindness and mutual support were overcome by vanity and self-absorption, a place where Nick could find an explanation for the emotional chaos and madness that surrounded this case. Instead, he found all the markings of a warm and supportive family. The signs of tenderness permeating this quiet cottage on the lake were genuine—his instincts told him so. It was a place where love and mutual respect had once resided. *What happened? Who allowed Lucifer in here?* he asked himself silently.

Chapter 8

THE CONFESSION

In a sudden turn of events, Logan Hughes called Moynihan to his office and informed him that Lorraine Parker would enter a plea of guilty in the slaying of her husband. The district attorney would reduce the charge to second-degree homicide in exchange for her written and signed confession, which would include a detailed description of the events leading up to the murder.

Moynihan was dumbfounded. "When did she agree to this?"

"Last night. I told her that the evidence we had was enough to convict her of murder one and that she could make it easier for herself and her family if she admitted to the whole affair and avoided the death penalty."

"Her lawyer consented to this?"

"Reluctantly, but yes. Now I need you to reconcile the evidence with the truth. There's just a touch of chaos mixed into the reality of this tale, chaos that in the end could lead to a mistrial if the confession is not given precisely and without prejudice. I've outlined the evidence and circumstances that point relentlessly to Lorraine as the murderer, but I want you to handle the interrogation and deposition, Red. It will be your job to validate her confession in a way that seals her fate without airing the lurid details that a trial would otherwise make public."

Moynihan opened the envelope and scanned the pages with some mistrust. It had been just two weeks earlier that Hughes had advocated the death penalty if Lorraine refused to name a coconspirator. Now she was being shown the middle path to a life sentence at the state prison in Framingham, with possible early release for good behavior.

"I'll read this over tonight, and if I have any questions I'll call you in the morning. In the meantime, I'll plan to see Lorraine on Wednesday."

"That's good, Red. I think we can both agree that this is the best course, and I am certain Judge McWilliams will concur. He has indicated to me that he has no desire to prolong this case."

.   .   .

Moynihan arrived at the Lawrence Correctional Facility at eight o'clock on Wednesday morning. A stenographer was present, setting up equipment for the interview, as he approached the interrogation room, and he could see that Lorraine was already there and seated. She was not wearing a prison issue jumpsuit but had on a pretty, light cotton housedress and a pearl necklace, earrings, and heels. She looked remarkably vibrant for someone who was about to confess to having murdered her husband. But hadn't she been the antithesis of a cold-blooded killer right from the beginning? Hadn't he, Red Moynihan, believed in her innocence in the face of mounting evidence? And now here it was—he would, this very morning, extract from Lorraine Parker a confession of one of the most brutal murders in Amesbury history, as all the while she appeared before him wearing a pretty, everyday, light cotton housedress.

Moynihan entered the room and informal introductions were exchanged all around, though he knew, at least by name, everyone except for the prison matron standing by the door.

He smiled faintly. "Good morning, Lorraine."

"Good morning to you, Mr. Moynihan, though I wish it were under more promising circumstances."

Red nodded reflectively.

"Lorraine, I want to establish first that the statement that you are about to give is offered voluntarily and that you have not been coerced in any way, as provided by the Fifth Amendment privilege against self-incrimination. Do you so swear that any statements you make today are truthful and given of your own free will?"

"I do so swear."

Moynihan glanced down at the notes that Hughes had given him, then put them aside—he knew by heart the line of interrogation he must take.

"Let us begin from the night of April tenth. Lorraine, tell me about the argument and what precipitated it."

"Al came home unexpectedly that night. He wasn't feeling well, and his supervisor sent him home early. The kids were at my parents', so we were alone. I had been entertaining a friend earlier, a gentleman with whom I had become infatuated—someone who stirred in me an uncontrollable passion. Al could see the telltale signs. If the truth be known, I think he suspected all along that I had strayed from our marriage vows, but he didn't want to face up to it; he was in a state of denial until that very moment. He asked me if I had remained faithful, and I said no, that I had fallen in love with another man. He wanted to know if the man and I had had intercourse, and I just stared at him and he could see the answer in my eyes. It was at that moment that he fell apart. He broke down in tears and pleaded with me to end the affair. He kept on saying, 'What about the children? Think about them!' He was on his knees, begging for contrition for the longest time, when just as suddenly he regained his composure

and began lecturing me, telling me that I had commit-
ted a mortal sin and that I would be condemned to
eternal damnation if I didn't repent and make our marriage whole again. We argued some more, until I told
him that I could never go back into a marriage that I
had come to detest. I told him that I would protect our
children at all costs, but that it was time to move on,
that I had to begin a new chapter in my life."

Lorraine paused and cast her eyes downward as
her voice trembled slightly from the memory. Moynihan poured water into a glass and offered it to her.
It was a chance for her to collect herself in the act of
confession. She had to follow the script, if only her interrogator would oblige. The water relieved her thirst
and reset her composure; her mind was sharp and co-
hesive in purpose.

"What happened next, Lorraine? What propelled
the argument—the confrontation, if you will—toward
its violent conclusion?"

"Al regressed to tears again. He was wailing in-
comprehensibly, and he fell back into his chair, head
in hands, heaving up and down against his knees. It
was pitiful seeing him dissolve into such a wretched
soul. Here was a man who once knew how to deal with
adversity falling apart before my eyes. I went to the
kitchen to get a damp washcloth so that he could wipe
away the tears, and when I returned, I saw the gun.
I don't know where it came from, whether it was in

the drawer of the end table or if it was in his jacket the whole time, but there it was, grasped coldly in his hand. I cannot remember exactly what was said, but I'm sure I told him to put it away; it was a crazy thing to have a loaded gun in the house when he was so emotionally distraught. He stared back at me with a look, a look that screamed both despair and rage. I pleaded with him again to put down the gun, when he slowly raised it to his head. 'Is this what you want?' he said, 'I can blow my brains out and end it all. Then you'll be free and you can spit on my grave.' I remember thinking what an odd expression that was, when I heard the gun make a cocking sound. So I just reacted out of instinct—I yelled something and lunged at him. All I could think was, I had to get the gun out of the house, outside, where I could throw it in the lake, where it wouldn't be a danger to me or to him.

"We struggled and pushed and I screamed again; then, in an instant, I heard the shot. It didn't seem that loud, but it was startling, like an unexpected collision that sends a prickly shock wave down your spine. Al slumped backward into the chair again. He didn't say anything, but a gurgling sound came from deep inside his throat. His eyes remained open in an expression of disbelief, as though he had been caught in a complete surprise. I'm sure I spoke to him, but I have no idea what I said. I might have asked if he was all right, until I saw the wound: a bloody pockmark on his face, just below the eye. I still had the washcloth in my hand, so

I began wiping the blood away, when I realized it was from the gunshot. I went numb, I was traumatized, and I sat down on the floor and wanted to cry, but I couldn't or wouldn't. I don't know why."

"Who then . . . who did you call to help you dispose of the body?"

"Why, I didn't call anyone. I just sat on the floor for the longest time, before I started to think about what I must do to protect my children—to protect them from the shame and the stigma that would follow them all their lives if they heard that I had driven their father to the brink of suicide, and all the tawdry lies that would inevitably follow. So I dragged him to the back of the cottage and I wrapped his body in chicken wire. I found some electrical wire in Al's shop and attached a cinder block to each of his legs. I used all my strength to boost him into the trunk of the convertible, and I drove to the Rocks Village Bridge and lifted him over the rail and into the river. I went back to the cottage and cleaned up the awful, bloody mess until daybreak."

There was a long silence before Moynihan spoke. "Lorraine, it is impossible for me to believe that you have the strength or the fortitude to heft a one-hundred-fifty-five-pound man trussed with cinder blocks into the trunk of your car, much less over a four-foot railing at the Rocks Village Bridge, without help from anyone else."

"There have been stranger tales, Mr. Moynihan. We've all heard the story of the California mother who lifted a car off her child who was pinned to the ground in the aftermath of an accident. It's the adrenaline and the mind over matter that take control in a crisis, and that's what happened here—I have no doubt. No, Mr. Moynihan, there was no accomplice."

More silence.

"What did you do with the gun?"

"What do you mean? You found the gun the day you were at the cottage with your team of inspectors. They took it away as evidence—why, you even gave me a receipt."

"The markings on test bullets fired from that pistol were not a match with those we removed from the overstuffed chair, Lorraine. There had to be another gun."

Lorraine looked confused, as though she were acting in a stage play that had gone off script. She responded with a wavering voice, ad-libbed. "You are asking me something unexpected, Chief Moynihan, and I have no idea what it is I'm supposed to say. I have no idea, honestly."

·   ·   ·

Even though a confession was given, a grand jury was necessary to hear the evidence before a trial could be convened and a decision handed down by Judge McWilliams. Such confidential hearings were designed to give the jurors as much flexibility as possible, and the rules of evidence permitted far more leeway than would be allowed at a criminal trial. It was the prosecutor's job to explain the law to the jurors and help them reach a finding. But the jurors had the power to view almost any kind of evidence they wanted and to interrogate anyone they liked, and therein lay the risk. Logan Hughes was uneasy; Moynihan's interrogation and Lorraine's confession had not gone as seamlessly as he had hoped, and too many unanswered questions had been exposed. Then, in an inexplicable turn of events, Hughes revealed that he had asked his assistant district attorney, Stephen Pratt, to present the evidence to the grand jury, while he would decide what evidence would be introduced from outside the courtroom—behind the scenes. Eleven witnesses were called to appear, including Moynihan; Alvin Parker, Sr.; medical examiner Stuart Manikas; State Police Lieutenant Frank Rizzo; several neighbors from Lake Attitash, whose names were kept confidential; and the ephemeral Arthur J. Flynn.

The hearing was into its second week in late August and by all indications would be concluded before Labor Day. Although testimony took place behind closed doors, Nick rarely allowed secrecy rules to get in the way of a good story, so he acquired, through a nameless source, copies of transcripts from the proceedings. He learned that Artie Flynn had invoked his Fifth Amendment rights and refused to answer any of the grand jury's questions—a strategy that undoubtedly led to greater suspicions than either the prosecution or Artie sought. The medical examiner was closely questioned about stab wounds reportedly observed on the thorax of the victim. He described them as superficial but provided no explanation for their cause. At one point, Mr. Pratt interjected that Mrs. Parker denied there was any stabbing involved, and that since the puncture wounds were not the cause of death, the district attorney had no interest in pursuing that line of investigation. Of a more prurient interest was the jury's questioning of several members of the Lake Attitash community at length about the alleged sex parties, but only one of the witnesses admitted to participating, and the more lurid testimony was struck from the record. The missing murder weapon was never addressed, and Lorraine's confession was conspicuously given scant mention in the transcription.

Nick was brooding: "There's no question the grand jury is going to indict her for murder—they'd indict a ham sandwich if the DA pressed them. But it's hard to sort out the truth here. Any way you look at it, Lorraine was a perfidious spouse and a schemer, but that doesn't necessarily add up to premeditated murder. And I don't trust Artie Flynn for one minute. He's at least a party to this criminal investigation, and he's getting off scot-free. But if his tale about the second bullet is true, there's another trail that's gone unexamined. Finally, there's our friend the Baron, who was a leading character in this whole production until suddenly he wasn't.

Jade said, "The transcript makes it seem as though Lorraine was never really grilled on any of the discrepancies in in her story, like the second head wound or the missing pistol. That's unlike Moynihan—he's thorough and persistent, if nothing else. I think I'll wait until the DA releases her confession—that should make for some interesting reading. After that, I'll approach him for a statement."

Three days passed without any news from the district attorney's office, and Lorraine Parker's confession remained sealed, until the assistant DA, Stephen Pratt, announced Lorraine Parker's indictment at a brief news conference outside the Salem courthouse.

"Thanks to the efforts of a three-month-long investigation," he said, "a grand jury has indicted Lorraine Parker for murder in the second degree—and without the evidence of a murder weapon," he added pointedly, "the death penalty is out of the question." He offered few other details and made no mention of a coconspirator; the prosecuting attorney departed the podium almost as quickly as he had arrived, leaving the press in a state of bewilderment.

Chapter 9

FRONT PAGE

Grand Jury Returns Indictment in Lorraine Parker Case: DA Suppresses Confession, Saying Details Are Too Sordid

The headline was predictable, as was the still-unanswered question of complicity. The decision to seal the confession, however, was an unexpected shock that let down a legion of *Daily News* readers famished for a compelling ending to a case that had captivated the public's imagination for months. Nick and Jade contributed equally to the article but took little satisfaction in the result. It was like covering a baseball game that ended in a tie, with no extra innings. Beyond that, it didn't seem as though justice had been served by any measure. A trial date was set for October, but that was perfunctory; Lorraine would plead guilty to second-degree murder, and Judge McWilliams would sentence her to life at the women's state prison in Framingham.

When the time came, Moynihan was Lorraine's noble sentinel. He whispered words of encouragement and gave her advice on how to behave once she was in-side the prison. "It's kind of like a big high school," he said, "but you have to watch your back." To shield her from the more violent population, he would do what he could to secure her a good job as a prison clerk, in view of her previously unblemished record and edu-cation, and when her time came to appear before the parole board, whenever that day might arrive, he would support her petition.

In the meantime, another jury returned secret indictments accusing Arthur Flynn of three counts of adultery: one with Lorraine Parker, two with a second, unnamed woman. The indictments had been returned nearly a month earlier but had been a closely guarded secret until Logan Hughes had announced them at a pretrial hearing. According to Jade's byline, Lorraine Parker's attorney expressed surprise when informed of Flynn's arrest, and rumors were rampant—one claimed that a girlfriend of Flynn said he had boasted that he'd killed Alvin Parker, but nothing came of it. At his trial, Flynn was found guilty of the morals charges and sen-tenced to one year for each of three counts, to be served consecutively.

.   .   .

A week or so later, a forty-five-foot Chris-Craft motor yacht with a sleek, gleaming white hull, varnished mahogany deck, and broad canvas dodger entered

Newburyport Harbor at about 5:30 P.M., seeking suitable anchorage on the north side of the channel, just below the girder bridge. The vessel flew an ensign from somewhere in the Caribbean, and the name on the transom read *Nautika*. She was a rumrunner, so the port of call was vaguely familiar.

By nightfall, Andros Farkas waited expectantly for his fugitive passenger, Arthur Flynn, to board. They were strange bedfellows, these two, bound by a messy affair that could expose Farkas to unnecessary diplomatic complications should Flynn decide to cut a deal with the district attorney. The less said, the better. As for Artie, the Baron represented his "get out of jail free" card, so he was more than happy to let bygones be bygones. So Farkas acted swiftly, surreptitiously securing Flynn's release, pending an appeal, and by daybreak they were navigating their way down the Intracoastal Waterway toward Florida, where a freighter bound for South America waited and the transfer would be made.

.   .   .

On November 27, Logan Hughes drove home from Boston, where Holy Cross closed out a disappointing football season by losing to Boston College, 31–13. The score didn't matter so much, as the game represented a chance to cheer on his beloved Crusaders with friends from a different time and place—an escape from the chaos that had enveloped him for the last five months. There was a full moon rising as he slowed the Ford sedan to a stop on the bridge at Rocks Village. He exited the car and stood at the rail to gaze at the reflection that shone dimly across the Merrimack. *The river is like life itself*, he thought. *It moves along, occasionally banging against the rocks. It may tumble over some obstacle, but that is not the end. It swirls around, then picks up the current and continues its journey to the sea.*

He whispered something and crossed himself, before reaching into his pocket for the reason for his stop. Grasping a nickel-plated revolver by its barrel, he launched the weapon as far as he could into the night, until a quiet splash confirmed its destination.

Chapter 10
EPILOGUE

The Lorraine Parker case fascinated Ian Ridgeway from the day he first learned about the murder and trial until the day he completed his education and entered the field of journalism. This was not his great-uncle's world of noisy newsrooms and printing presses. He was a freelance writer contributing to numerous news websites for fifteen cents per word in a cyber-universe where social media spread information in an instant. But the independence allowed him the time and the patience to conduct his own analysis of the case more than six decades removed, and he hoped to chronicle his findings by writing a book. He found and studied his uncle's notes, and he interviewed as many of the individuals in the investigation as he could track down, though most of the key players either were dead or living with faded memories. He learned that Red Moynihan had taken a position as police chief for a small town in central Maine. His nephew said the Parker case always haunted Moynihan and the change seemed like a means of escape, but it wasn't. He died from complications related to Alzheimer's in 1996. Logan Hughes, the mercurial District Attorney was playing golf when he collapsed and died from a heart attack in 1962. Amazingly, Ian was able to track Artie Flynn's escape route all the way to Venezuela where he worked in the oil fields through the late 1950s, but after that the trail went cold. The so-called Baron left no trail whatsoever and try as he might Ian could not even confirm his existence. As for the Clique, the infamous group of adulterers, they faded into obscurity when the cultural revolution of the 1960s made such escapades tame by comparison.

That left the ultimate prize in Ian's investigation unchallenged. In 1963 the Governor's Council voted 7-2 to reduce Lorraine Parker's life sentence to twenty-two years to life. Because she had already served more than one-third of the sentence, she was immediately eligible for parole, and after nine years of confinement in Framingham State Prison, Lorraine was released. Newspaper accounts at the time said that the town of Amesbury showed compassion upon her return, but after a time she moved to be near her children, living in Florida and later New Hampshire, until she made a final move back to Amesbury to be with her grand-daughter. She was now in her nineties and alert, but in the advanced stages of cancer. Her family was understandably protective and mistrustful of the media, but Ian had a gentle persistence and friendly manner that won them over. Whatever he wrote, they were certain, would be fair and empathetic. He visited with Lorraine once a week for six weeks, testing her memory for names and places that surrounded the episode. She was frail but friendly, and her eyes revealed an irresistible charm whenever she shared a pleasant memory from the past. She enjoyed the company, and Ian earned some measure of trust, so he decided to ask the question that had captivated so many locals for so many years. It was, he said, a way to put to rest the endless prattle that had dogged her family for decades. All he was asking for was a name; he was sure he could piece together motive and opportunity if only the name of her accomplice or lover was known.

Lorraine would consider it—she knew life was coming to an end, and she could either take her secrets to the grave or confide them to Ian, who she thought would regard her story with honesty and respect. They talked around the subject at every visit, even as her health declined rapidly and her speech became more and more difficult.

One day, he gave her a reporter's notepad and a pencil that he fastened to it with a string. "If you decide that it is best not to reveal these things, then I will understand—no hard feelings," he said with a smile. "But should you decide that it is praiseworthy in some way, that a final disclosure deserves merit, just write it all here, in this notebook, so that your story concludes in your own words, as *your* declaration of the truth." It was their last conversation.

.   .   .

Lorraine Parker lay quietly on the chaise lounge, sunlight peering through the blinds of her bedroom window. She could hear voices and laughter outside as schoolchildren cut through the yard on a warm spring day. She reached to pull the day blanket up around her neck, but it felt heavy and her arms trembled as she raised them into the air in a curious way. She breathed deeply. There was no pain, so she raised herself up so that she was half sitting. There was a scent in the air, most likely from the lilacs that bloomed outside her window, she decided. She took another breath, when the air suddenly felt thick and a rasp came from within her chest while an unfamiliar tingle ran up and down her limbs. The room took on an eerie hush. She thought to call out to her granddaughter, but the sensation passed and she was breathing easily again.

Her eyelids felt heavy, so she closed them and a dim presence gathered at the edge of her consciousness. She dreamed for a minute or two, or maybe it was an hour—she wasn't sure—but the dream revealed what she must do. It was all so clear to her now. Her head turned, and she reached for the notebook on the bed stand. She marveled at the thinness of her fingers as they ran across the spiral spine. She grasped the pencil with her usual open grip, but as sunlight faded from the room, her eyes no longer perceived the page before her; her hands loosened peacefully, and the notebook and pencil fell away into her lap, then slid silently to the floor.

THE END

ABOUT THE AUTHOR

Arthur H. Veasey III was born and raised in Haverhill, Massachusetts. He was educated at Haverhill Public Schools and Governor Dummer Academy in nearby Byfield before completing his higher education at the University of Denver in Colorado. *Sweet Lorraine* is his third novella. Mr. Veasey also writes short stories and has contributed essays to numerous publications. He resides in West Newbury with his wife Susan and their golden retriever Schooner.

Made in the USA
Middletown, DE
16 November 2018